WORLD
Facto and Friends
Is it here?
Is it here?
Is it here?
MUSEUM
Is it here?
Is it here?
Ask Professor Facto
Discovery World can be anywhere!
OIC
OIC2

# Dinosaurs
## Back in Time

*by Jane Belk Moncure*
*illustrated by Linda Hohag*
*color by Lori Jacobson*

Distributed by CHILDRENS PRESS®
Chicago, Illinois

*Grateful appreciation is expressed to Elizabeth Hammerman, Ed. D., Science Education Specialist, for her services as consultant.*

**Library of Congress Cataloging in Publication Data**

Moncure, Jane Belk.
Dinosaurs : back in time / by Jane Belk Moncure ; illustrated by Linda Hohag.
p. cm. — (Discovery world)
Summary: Visiting the Natural History Museum, Annie learns about dinosaurs from Professor Facto.
ISBN 0-89565-550-0
1. Dinosaurs—Juvenile literature. [1. Dinosaurs.] I. Hohag, Linda, ill. II. Title. III. Series.
QE862.D5M59 1990
567.9'1—dc20 89-38469
CIP
AC



1 2 3 4 5 6 7 8 9 10 11 12 R 99 98 97 96 95 94 93 92 91 90

# Dinosaurs
## Back in Time

DISCOVERY
with Professor
Hi ! I'm Professor Facto.
And we're his helpers !
OIC
OIC2
Where is Discovery World?
It can be anywhere—
anywhere at all.
It can be at a zoo,
a museum, or beside the sea.
It can be in a pond,
a library, or up in a tree.
All you need is curiosity.
It can be right at
your own back door.
All you need to do is EXPLORE!

*So come along and find out more about . . .*

*DINOSAURS!*

It's Dinosaur Day at the museum. Annie has been waiting a long time for this day.

"Where are they? Where are all the dinosaurs?" she asks Professor Facto.

"Right this way," he says, and off they go to Dinosaur Hall.

Guess what Annie sees?

A huge skeleton! "Wow!" says Annie.

"This is an Apatosaurus skeleton. It has more than 200 bones," says the professor.

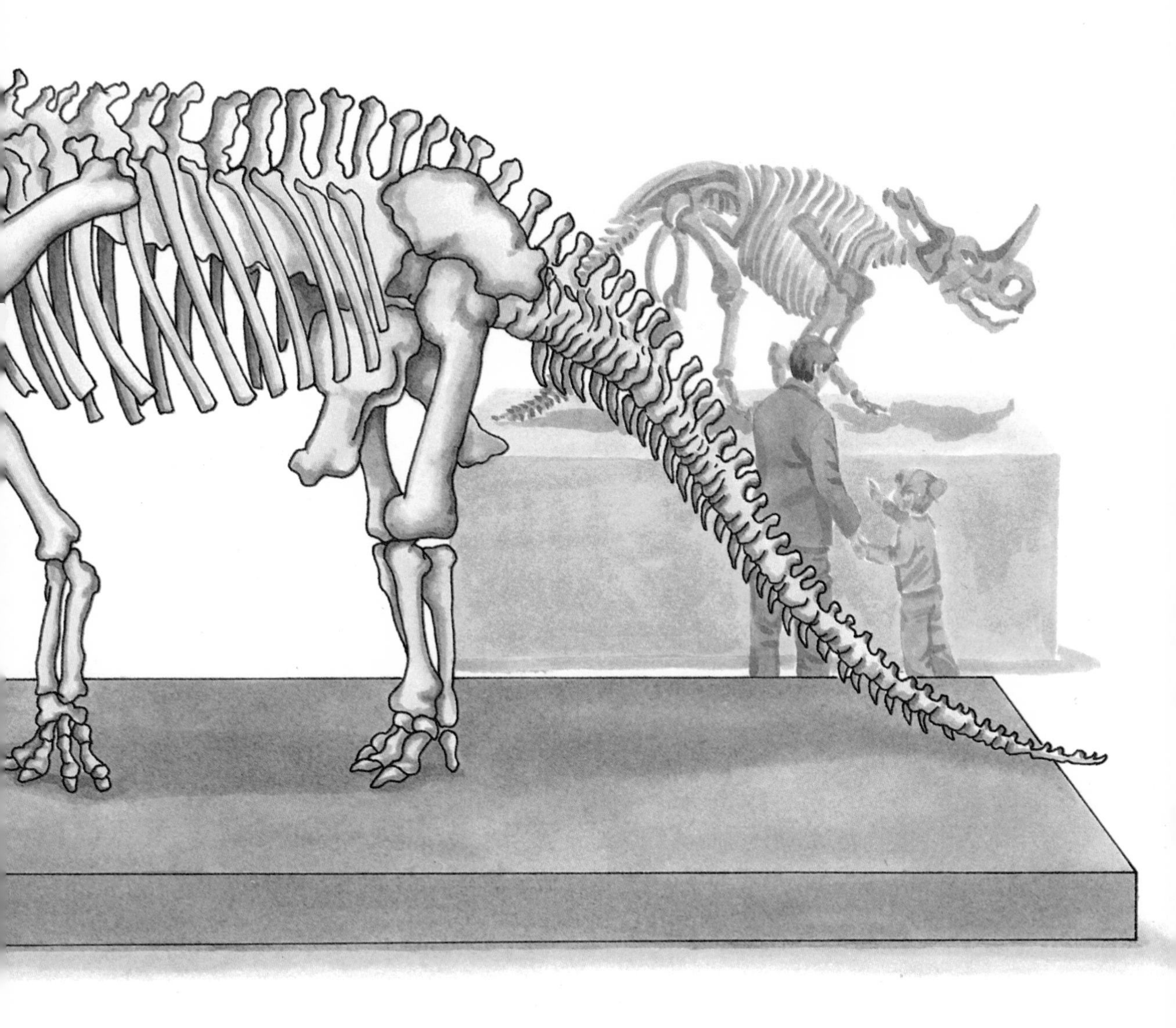

“It took scientists a long time to put them together. But once they had the skeleton, they could make a life-like model of the dinosaur.

“This is a model of an Apatosaurus.”
“He looks as big as a bus,” says Annie.
“He was even bigger,” says Professor Facto.

"That dinosaur looks as tall as a tree," says Annie.

"He was even taller," says Professor Facto.

"Some dinosaurs were big and tall. Some were very small."

"As small as a dog?" asks Annie.

"Even smaller," says Professor Facto.

"Some dinosaurs laid eggs in nests and brought food to their babies."

"Just like birds?" asks Annie.

"That's right," says Professor Facto.

"And many dinosaurs even protected their babies."

"How?" asks Annie.

"Well, they kept the babies in the center of the herd, away from danger."

"Did they have to protect them from this dinosaur with the horns?" asks Annie.

"No, he wouldn't hurt them. And he really needed his three helpful horns."

"How were they helpful?" asks Annie.

"We can find out," says the professor. "Put on your imagination cap, and we will take a pretend trip back in time."

"Good idea!" says Annie. She puts on the cap and ZIPPITY ZAP! They are back in the time of the dinosaurs.

Guess what they see? A huge Triceratops!

"Let's run and hide!" says Annie.

"Oh, no," says Professor Facto. "Triceratops won't hurt us. He eats only plants. We are safe."

“Do all dinosaurs eat plants?” asks Annie.

“Oh, no,” says Professor Facto. “Some dinosaurs are meat eaters.

“Here comes a meat eater now. It’s the terrible Tyrannosaurus Rex!”

"Look at those sharp teeth!" cries Annie.
"Run and hide, Triceratops!"
But Triceratops does not run and hide.

"Now you will find out how Triceratops uses his three helpful horns," says Professor Facto.

Just as Tyrannosaurus Rex is about to attack, Triceratops rams him—*thump bump*—with his horns. He knocks Tyrannosaurus Rex down.

While Tyrannosaurus Rex tries to get back up, Triceratops makes his escape.

"Now I know why Triceratops has three helpful horns!" says Annie.

"Oh dear, it is getting late," says Professor Facto. "Let's hurry back."

ZIP ZAP! Off with the caps,

and they are back at the museum.

"That pretend trip was fun!" says Annie. "Now I want to find out more about dinosaurs."

"You can," says Professor Facto. "There are lots of books about dinosaurs. You can pick one out for yourself."

"Thank you," says Annie as she waves good-bye.

Now Annie can explore some more. So can you!

## EXPLORE SOME MORE WITH PROFESSOR FACTO!

Scientists learn about dinosaurs by studying the things they left behind—bones, teeth, eggs, and even footprints. These things are called *fossils*. You can make your own "fossils." Here's how:

1. Cover the bottom of an aluminum pie pan with modeling clay, pressing it smooth.
2. Press different objects, such as shells, acorns, rocks, leaves, etc., into the clay and then remove them. You may even want to make a thumbprint in the clay.
3. Mix plaster of Paris and water, following the directions on the package. Pour this mixture over the clay and let it dry until it's very hard.
4. Carefully lift the plaster off of the clay.

What do you see? What can you tell about the things that left the prints? What do you think you could learn about dinosaurs by looking at the footprints they left behind?

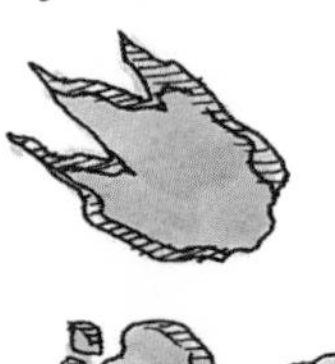
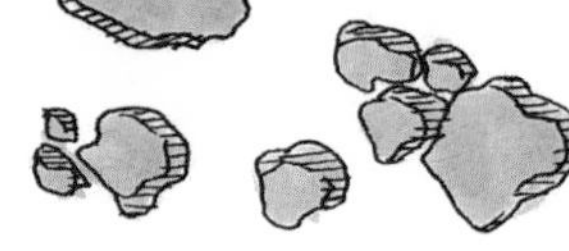

Everyone knows most dinosaurs were big, but how big is big? How many kids would it take to reach the top of a dinosaur? Try this to find out:

Tyrannosaurus was about 20 ft. (6 m) tall and 50 ft. (15 m) long. On a sidewalk, make 2 chalk marks 20 ft. apart. (Use a tape measure or yardstick to measure the distance.) Find out how many kids, lying head to toe, it takes to reach 20 ft. (You can also have one friend mark how many times you fit into that space.) Next measure 50 ft. on the sidewalk. Find out how many kids *long* the Tyrannosaurus was. You can find out the sizes of other dinosaurs and do the the same experiment.

## INDEX

Apatosaurus, 8-9, 10, 14
Brachiosaurus, 11
Compsognathus, 12
eggs, 13
experiments
  making "fossils," 30
  measuring dinosaurs, 31
fossils, 30
herding, 14
Maiasaura, 13
meat eaters, 20-21
nests, 13
plant eaters, 19-20
Triceratops, 15, 18-25
Tyrannosaurus Rex, 21-25, 31